Licensed exclusively to Top That Publishing Ltd
Tide Mill Way, Woodbridge, Suffolk, IP12 1AP, UK
www.topthatpublishing.com
Copyright © 2014 Tide Mill Media
All rights reserved
2 4 6 8 9 7 5 3 1
Manufactured in China

ISBN 978-1-78244-785-6

A catalogue record for this book is available from the British Library

Tatty Tractor
and
Big Yellow Truck

Splutter, rumble, crunch, croak!
Tatty Tractor starts with a puff of smoke.
Farmer Ruggles ploughs the ground,
But Tatty makes a groaning sound!

Splutter, rumble, crunch, croak!
Tatty Tractor rattles, shakes and chokes.
Sowing row upon row of seeds,
In mounds of earth, no sign of weeds!

Splutter, rumble, crunch, croak!
Tatty Tractor works hard by the big old oak.
Little shoots soon start to show,
See them grow ... and grow ... and grow!

Chugga, chug, chug!

Splutter, rumble, crunch, croak!
Tatty Tractor worked so hard he broke!
But Farmer Ruggles has a plan,
And fixes Tatty, clever man!

Chugga, chug, chug!

Splutter, rumble, crunch, croak!
Tatty Tractor starts with a puff of smoke.
His work is done, he's homeward bound.
He rumbles home with a chugga-chug sound.

Rumble, thunder, clatter, crash!
Collected rocks and rubble clash.
At the quarry, Big Yellow Truck drives around,
Making a noisy, busy sound.

Rumble, thunder, clatter, crash!
To the building site the truck must dash.
It tips up loads of rocks and stone,
So heavy that it starts to groan!

Rumble,
beep!

Rumble, thunder, clatter, crash!
The truck is filled with coal in a flash.
The cargo comes from mines so deep,
Rumble, rumble, beep, beep, beep!

Rumble, thunder, clatter, crash!
The truck drives through black smoky ash.
It loads its coal into the train,
And just in time, before it rains!

Rumble, thunder, clatter, crash!
The Big Yellow Truck is loud and brash!
Always moving heavy loads around,
With a rumble, beep and clatter–crash sound!

Rumble, beep!

To Neil and Andrew, with love.

X

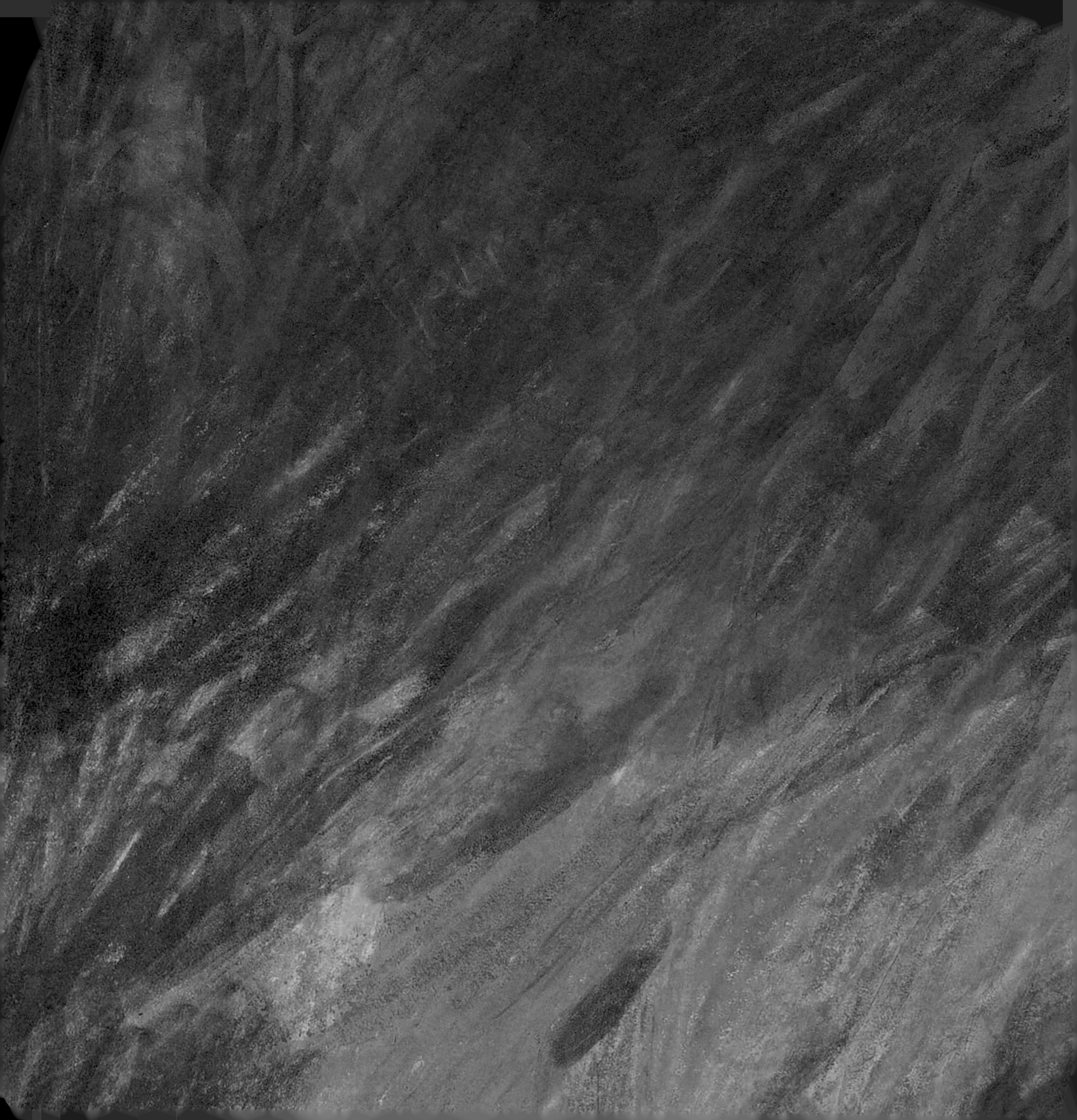

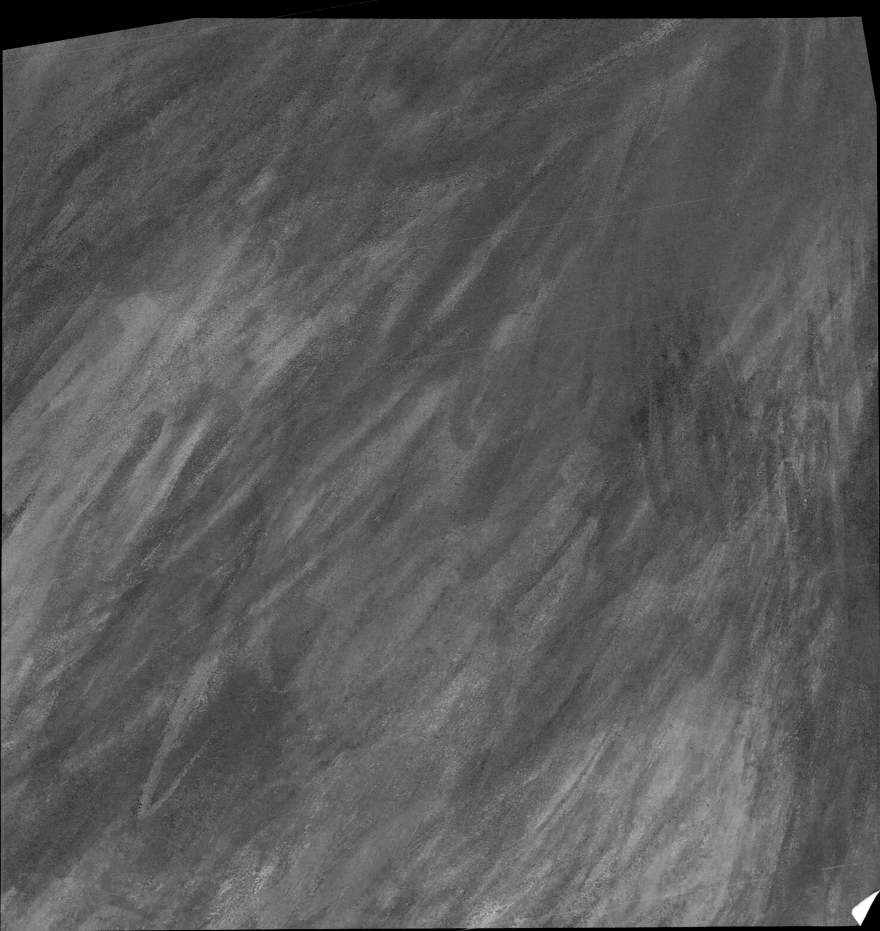

ISBN: 978-1-913339-48-7
Text copyright © Ian Eagleton 2023
Illustrations copyright © Jessica Knight 2023

RORY'S ROOM OF RECTANGLES

Written by Ian Eagleton

Illustrated by Jessica Knight

First published in the UK
2023 by Owlet Press

www.owletpress.com

Rory sat in class, watching the leaves dance around the playground in the whistling wind.

Mr Spencer-Smith was showing the class how to make Father's Day cards.

"You can make a card for your grown-ups at home or anyone special," he said. "I'm going to give mine to my husband." Everyone started to carefully paint their cards.

But not Rory. He DID NOT like Father's Day . . .

He still saw Dad every weekend. They played in the park,

fed the greedy ducks and pigeons,

and ate crispy, hot chips on the bench.

But now, Rory lived with Mum and her new boyfriend, Tony.

And THEY spent time painting, drawing,

and creating new, imaginary worlds.

Still, Rory missed seeing Dad every day. He wondered what Dad was doing when he wasn't there? And, who would Rory send HIS card to?

Confusion spilled from Rory as he covered his Father's Day card in angry swishes, flicks and swirls.

At home time, Rory ripped his card in half, stuffing it quickly into his coat pocket.

This Father's Day, Mum, Tony and Rory watched movies, ate popcorn, and played board games. But as it began to rain and the wind made the leaves twirl outside, Rory remembered the card hidden deep in his coat pocket. Wouldn't Dad be lonely on Father's Day?

Tony saw Rory's face change, and whispered, "I've been saving up some money for a rainy day. Come on, let's go out together, just you and me."

Tony's face looked kind and Mum nodded happily, so Rory took his hand, even though it felt a bit scary.

They went over bridges...

through dark tunnels...

and down into the noisy underground.

Where were they going?

Together, Tony and Rory wandered through long white corridors and around large rooms, looking at all kinds of wonderful paintings.

Some were delicate, shimmering with shapes, swirls and patterns.
"These are my dad's favourite," Tony explained. "He used to bring me here when I was little - we always loved these paintings."

But others were scary! Rory felt like he'd fallen into a nightmare
when he saw some of the strange painted worlds in front of him.

Rory loved the bright, loud and fierce art they saw too.
He felt like he'd seen it somewhere before.
Finally, Rory and Tony reached a room full of giant rectangles...

They were dazzling: full of broad strokes of colour, swishes,
flicks and swirls too, just like Rory had made at school!

Rory and Tony sat there, silent and still, for a long time.

"This room is my favourite," Tony said quietly.

"Why?" Rory asked, biting his lip.

"The paintings are so full of power and emotion,
but they're also quite sad as well, aren't they?"
Rory looked up at the rectangles, feeling like they
were reflecting his own feelings back to him.

He was happy to have Tony in his life now, but would Dad be angry about it?
Or maybe Dad would forget him altogether? Rory felt tears sting his eyes.
Just then, he felt Tony's hand on his shoulder...

"I guess life is like an art gallery, isn't it?" Tony said gently. "Sometimes it's full of happiness and joy, sometimes it's scary, and sometimes it's sad. But that's OK. Whatever you feel is OK."

They hugged for a long time, and the paintings seemed to wash over and around them.

"I've got one more thing to show you," Tony smiled, ruffling Rory's hair. "Come on!"

As the setting sun painted reds, blues and greys across the dusky sky, they waited outside the gallery ... Rory saw something ... someone in the distance ... DAD!

"I got a message from Tony to say you might like to see me," Dad smiled, shaking hands with Tony.
"This fell out of your coat pocket," said Tony.

It was Rory's card! "You don't ever have to feel torn between us," Tony said.
"Yes," Dad said, wiping something out of his eye, "you have BOTH of us now and we'll always
be here for you, whenever you need us." Rory jumped into Dad's arms and Dad held him tightly.

As they walked back through the quiet city, the clouds seemed to be bursting
with all kinds of colours and emotions, just like a beautiful painting.

Rory held hands with Dad on one side and Tony on the other,
while they swung him high into the deep red sky.
Rory smiled the happiest smile as the leaves danced
around them. Maybe he DID like Father's Day, after all.

Little Fern's First Winter

Jane Simmons

ORCHARD

For James, Maria and Gabriel

ORCHARD BOOKS
338 Euston Road, London NW1 3BH
Orchard Books Australia
Level 17/207 Kent Street, Sydney, NSW 2000

First published in 2000 by Orchard Books
First published in paperback in 2001
This edition published in 2010

ISBN 978 1 40830 499 0

Text and illustrations © Jane Simmons 2000

A CIP catalogue record for this book is available from the British Library.

1 3 5 7 9 10 8 6 4 2

Printed in Singapore

Orchard Books is a division of Hachette Children's Books, an Hachette UK Company.
www.hachette.co.uk

"The snow is coming!" said Ma Rabbit.

"What's snow?" said Fern.

"Lovely fluffy stuff when it settles, but very very cold," said Ma. "Go and play with Bracken while I change the hay."

Fern and Bracken hopped and
flipped and giggled together.
"Let's play hide and seek,"
said Fern. "I'll hide first."
"And I'll count," said
Bracken. "1, 2, 3, 4..."

Fern looked for somewhere to hide.
All the birds were swooping and chattering.
"The snow is coming! We must fly away!"
they squawked.

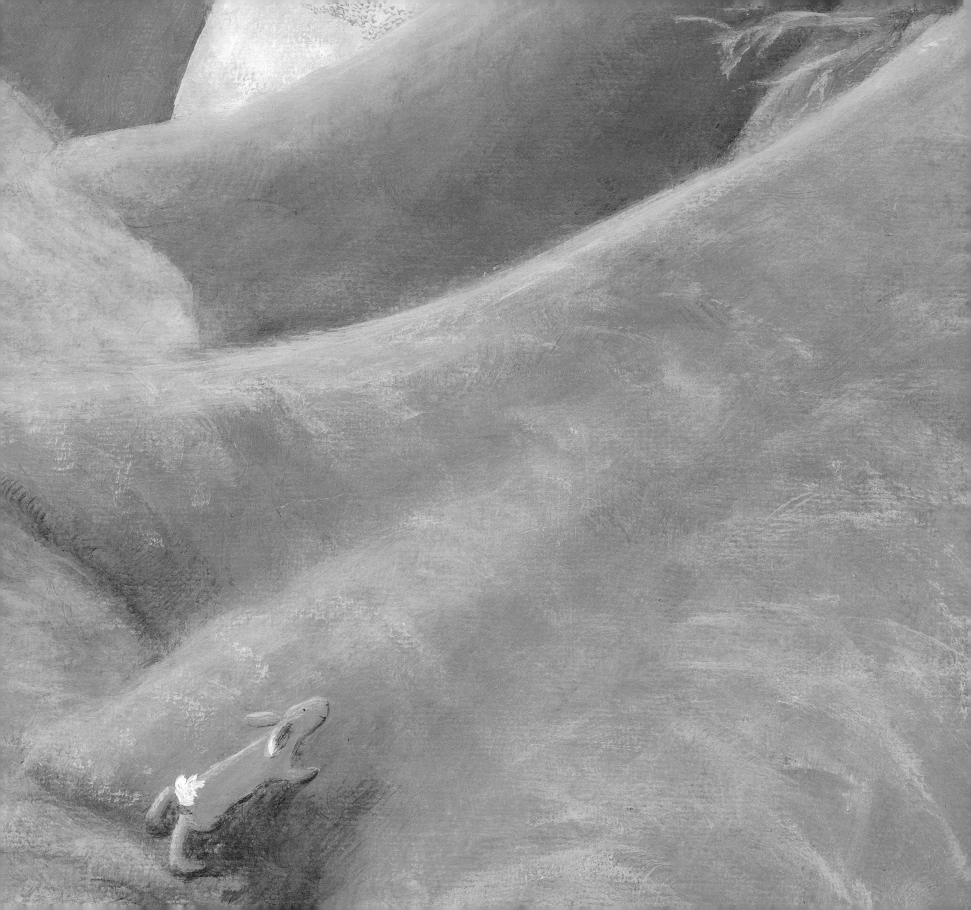

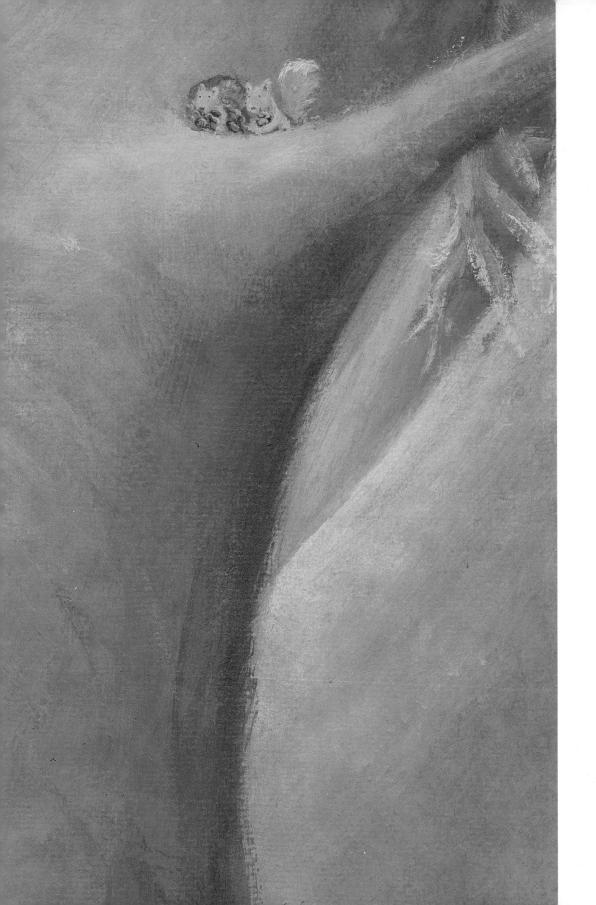

"Can I hide in your store?" asked Fern.

"No. The snow is coming! We need our store for our nuts," said squirrel.

So Fern hopped on.

"Can I hide in your nest?" Fern asked the mice. "The snow is coming! We need to sleep in our nest until it's warmer," they said.

"Can I hide with you?" she asked the beetles, but they just crept away.

Fern couldn't find anywhere to hide.

"Found you!" shouted Bracken. And they hopped and flipped and giggled together.

"Now it's your turn to hide," said Fern, and she started to count.

"1, 2, 3, 4, 5, 6, 7, 8 . . ."

"... 9, 10! I'm coming!"
she shouted.
Everything was quiet in the wood.

There were no birds in the sky . . .   no squirrels in the tree . . .

no mice in the grass . . .

no beetles under the leaves . . .

and no Bracken
anywhere!

Fern went down the burrow under the ground.

"Ma, have you seen Bracken?" asked Fern.

"No, dear," said Ma Rabbit. "I've been changing the hay."

So Fern went up the burrow and outside again.

"Bracken, where are you?" said Fern.
A chill wind whistled through the
silent wood. Fern shivered.
"Bracken!" she called. Something
cold and soft melted on her nose.

"Bracken!"

The whole wood changed.
Was this snow?
  "Where are you, Bracken?"
shouted Fern again.

BRACKEN!

"Fern," came a faint cry deep
in the snow. It was Bracken!
Fern dug and dug and dug . . .

and there at last was Bracken.

"What's happening?" he said, trembling.

"I think the snow has come," said Fern. "Ma says it's lovely when it settles."

And they huddled up as close as close could be until it stopped snowing.

And that night they all curled up as close
as close could be in the warm soft hay.

Then they hopped and flipped
and giggled in the fluffy cold snow.
   "Fern! Bracken!" called Ma Rabbit.
"Time to come in."